FRIENDLY LITTLE
JONATHAN

Dorothy and Marguerite Bryan

DODD, MEAD & COMPANY

NEW YORK

TO MICHAEL WHO TAUGHT
JONATHAN HOW TO BEHAVE.

Friendly Little Jonathan

Once there was a friendly little puppy named Jonathan, who grew up to be

a friendly little dog.
He liked everything and
everybody.

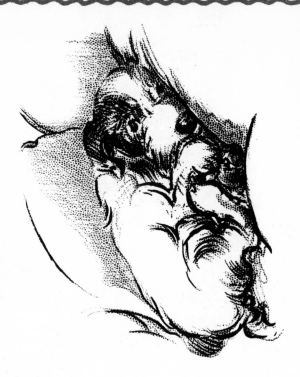

Friendly little Jonathan liked hot weather because then he could stretch out on his back in the soft dust under the blossoms.

But he liked cold weather, too, when he could curl up tightly on a soft cushion.

Friendly little Jonathan
liked the cosy cook and —

he liked what the cook cooked.

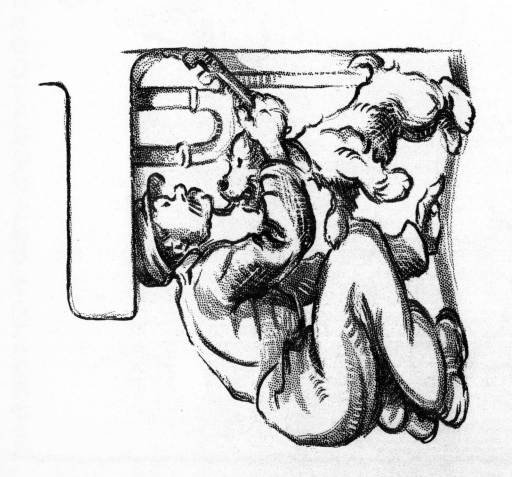

He liked the lean, lank plumber with his turned-down moustache, too. He folded up under the kitchen sink and was so VIO-LENTLY surprised when Jonny leaped up to love him.

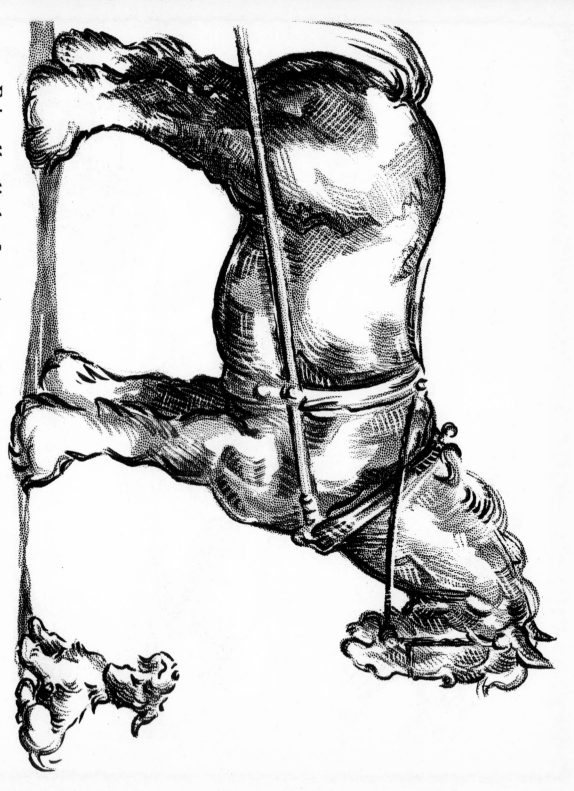

Friendly little Jonathan admired Moses, the enormous milk-wagon horse. There was so much of Moses to admire.

He found Dottie, the snappy
small donkey pleasant, too.
Dottie usually kicked —

or p-u-l-l-e-d back —

or just stood when people wanted
her to do anything special.

But Dottie made a fine little patch of shade where Jonathan rested on his long, sunny trip across the pasture.

Jonny liked Slow-Molasses Rastus, the yard man, who raked up great heaps of leaves — and then when Jonny had the leaves all tossed apart, amiably raked them together again.

Then he liked the fluffy yellow ducklings who came running when they saw him. He was popular with the ducklings.

But he liked the great roaring lion
at the Zoo.

And the lion seemed to like friendly little Jonathan. Now if a little dog liked a great lion and, more than that, if a great lion liked a little dog, you can see what a friendly dog Jonathan was.

Best of all Jonathan loved Janey.

He loved her so much that he let her put her aunt's new hats on him—and that is a great deal for a little dog to do.

Jonny's whiskered face did look funny under some of those hats—especially the tip-tilted ones.

SO friendly little Jonathan liked everybody. And everybody he met could not help liking friendly little Jonathan.

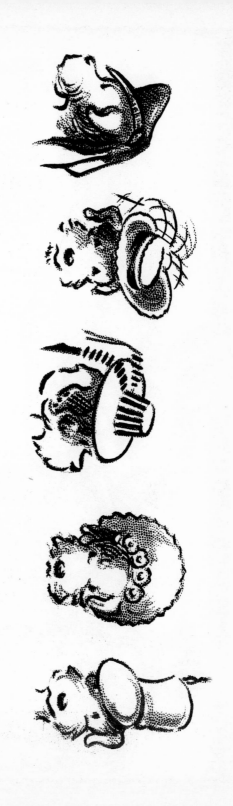

When Jonny went walking down the street any fine day, it was —"Morning, Little Fellow!" "Hi, Jonny!" and "Yea, Jonny!" and

"Good little Jonathan!" all along the way.

Even with all the clothes she had to wash, when Rastus' Mammy saw Jonathan passing

by she called out, "Come, hop in and I'll scrub you, too." But Jonny didn't like to linger around soapsuds. He just slipped along.

Soon he was stepping out gaily again.

How could any one help liking a nice, friendly little white dog like that?

Although some people did think he was rather a silly little dog to expect to be friends with *everybody*.

Well, a new dog moved to Jonathan's town.
He was a big dog. And what a face that dog had! It was so

terrific that when he opened his mouth to bark everyone around ran for home.

One afternoon Janey and Jonny went for a walk—up the street

and down the street.

Suddenly —G-r-r-r—w-o-o-f!!!
Chickens and ducks flew by!

G - R - R — R — W - O - O - F ! ! !

There was the big dog, coming towards them! Jonathan stiffened. He stepped in front of Janey. It was surprising how he knew how to frown—although his nice little face did have quite a time fixing itself that way at first. Friendly little Jonathan looked positively *un*friendly.

The big dog was so surprised to see a dog's *face* coming towards him, instead of a dog's *tail* running away from him, that he stopped short.

Jonathan started walking towards the big dog, still' frowning.

He came closer—and *closer*—

and CLOSER—

until finally he was right under the big dog's chin! And then—

Friendly little Jonathan reached up and licked that homely face! After all, he could not help having such a face! The big dog was astonished.

He did not know quite what to do about it. No one had ever dared be *friendly* with him before. Finally he decided to wag his tail about it.

Jonny was not so silly. After all, it is more fun to be friendly than fierce — as long as you are not afraid. At least, that is the way with friendly little Jonathan — and everybody likes *him*.